Apartment for Rent

Distributed to schools and libraries
in Canada by
SAUNDERS BOOK CO.
Box 308
Collingwood, Ontario, Canada L9Y 3Z7
(800) 461-9120

ISBN 089565-742-2
Library of Congress Cataloging-in-Publication Data
available upon request

Apartment

for Rent

A Lulu and Banana Story

author: Lionel Koechlin
illustrator: Annette Tamarkin Hatwell

The Child's World
Mankato, Minnesota

Banana is a cat.

Banana lives in town.

Once upon a time he was an explorer,
but he's given up traveling.

Banana is in retirement.

Lulu is a mouse.

Lulu was born in the country.

Lulu is taking the train to go to town and go to school with the big mice.

Banana lives in a little room all cluttered with souvenirs.

Lulu says goodbye to her parents. Her mother says,

"Be careful now, and stay away from the cafés."

Her father says:

"Be careful what you spend, because we have no more savings."

Banana is looking all over the place for his right shoe. He says to himself, "Yesterday I lost my necktie; this mess can't continue. I will have to move."

He thought for a moment, then added, "Of course, with the housing shortage, you can't find anything to rent these days."

Lulu is wondering:

"Wherever shall I sleep tonight, if I can't find an apartment?"

"Hurrah!" shouts Banana, "there's an ad in the paper at last! 'For rent, two sunny rooms, fully equipped kitchen, reasonable rent. Can be viewed today, 7 Rintintin Street.'"

Banana jumps into a cab. "I hope I'm the first one there," he thinks to himself.

Lulu checks the city map and decides to walk to Rintintin Street.

Outside 7 Rintintin Street there's already a line: a rabbit, a skunk, and a dog.

Banana hopes they won't like the apartment.

Lulu got lost for a while. She asked the way from a swallow who was a stranger to the area, and then a turkey misdirected her.

A nightingale is showing the apartment.

The rabbit goes up the stairs.

The rabbit comes back down and says, "Sure, the kitchen is equipped, but there's a family of roosters in the apartment below, and I like to sleep until noon."

The nightingale says,

"Please go up, Mrs. Dog."

The dog comes back down and says,

"The apartment is certainly sunny, but there's a magpie living on the same floor with her mother and her grandmother; I don't want to get my jewelry stolen!"

The nightingale says:

"If you please, Mr. Skunk."

The skunk comes back down and says,

"The rent is reasonable but there's a pair of pigs living right overhead."

The nightingale says,

"After you, Mr. Cat."

Banana says, "I'll live in this room and in the other one I'll put all my souvenirs away neatly. I hope my neighbors aren't allergic to cat hair."

The nightingale says,

"Please be so good as to make out your check to me, and I'll give you the keys."

Banana has a place of his own at last. Through the windows he gazes at the landscape that he'll soon know by heart.

In the distance there's a funny-looking roof that reminds him of houses in Africa.

But there's somebody ringing the bell.

"Good morning, Sir, I'd like to see the apartment, please," says Lulu.

"It's already taken, you poor little thing, and I'll be all moved in by tonight."

A tear rolls slowly down Lulu's cheek, and then she breaks into sobs.

Through her tears Lulu explains that she feels all alone in the world, that she'll have to go to a hotel and that she doesn't have much money.

Overhearing her story, the two pigs, the rooster
family and the magpies come out of their apartments.

To cheer Lulu up, the two pigs give her a piggy bank.
The magpies sing a song. The roosters give her a big
chef's hat.

Overcome, Banana offers to share his apartment with Lulu:

"Pick the room you'd like the best."

"I don't know how to thank you," cries Lulu, "but I'm sure an idea will come to me, sooner or later."

THE CHILD'S WORLD LIBRARY

THE LOVE AFFAIR OF MR. DING AND MRS. DONG

LULU AND THE ARTIST

THE MAGIC SHOES

THE NEXT BALCONY DOWN

OLD MR. BENNET'S CARROTS

THE RANGER SMOKES TOO MUCH

RIVER AT RISK

SCATTERBRAIN SAM

THE TALE OF THE KITE

TIM TIDIES UP

TOMORROW WILL BE A NICE DAY

THE TREE POACHERS